If You Were a Penguin

If You Were

a Penguin

Wendell and Florence Minor

Katherine Tegen Books
An Imprint of HarperCollins*Publishers*

If you were a penguin,
what could **you** do?

You could fly underwater

or sing a duet.

You could live on
the land but

get really
wet.

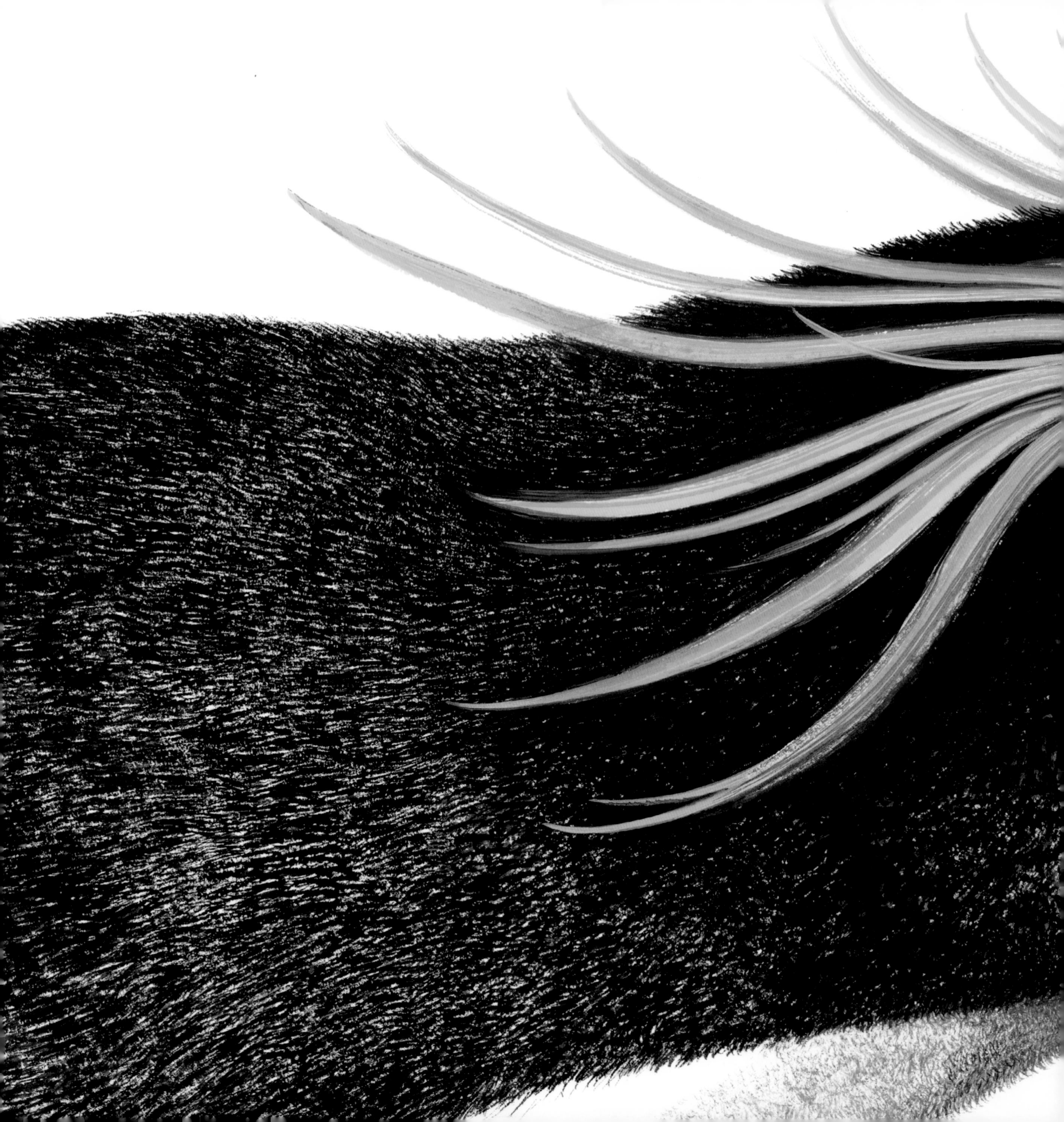

You could

wear a tuxedo

or make

funny faces.

You could go for a swim in *warm*

or **cold** places.

You could live
underground

or on top
of the ice.

Penguin pals all around

make it twice as nice!

You could have
funny names,

like Chinstrap and Gentoo.

You could learn to toboggan—

woo-hoo!!

You could wear **fancy feathers**
in dry or wet weather.

You could eat **squids** and **fishes**
without any dishes.

But here's a surprise for me and for *you*—
penguins do lots of things

that *you* can do too!

Penguin Fun Facts

Penguins can sleep standing up, sitting in water, lying down, or even perched in a tree!

Penguins can "fly" underwater as fast as twenty-five miles per hour.

Penguins look very graceful in the water. They waddle when they are on land, but they have very good posture!

Galápagos penguins hold their flippers out to keep cool and also to keep their feet from getting sunburned!

Some penguins can dive a thousand feet or more underwater and stay submerged for up to twenty-five minutes.

Each species of penguin has its own unique voice, and parents know the sound of their own chick.

Most adult penguins swallow their food whole.

Penguins talk to each other with vocal signals and by bowing, gesturing, and waving their flippers.

The largest penguin of the seventeen species of penguins, the emperor, can stand up to three and a half feet tall and can weigh from forty to ninety pounds.

The fairy penguin is the smallest penguin. It is only sixteen to seventeen inches tall and weighs about two pounds.

Adult Adélie penguins look like they are wearing tuxedos.

Because of the black stripe across its chin, a chinstrap penguin looks like it is always smiling!

Visit these websites for more fun facts about penguins!

www.nationalgeographic.com
www.buschgardens.org
www.penguinworld.com
www.seabirds.org

Do You Know Your Penguins?

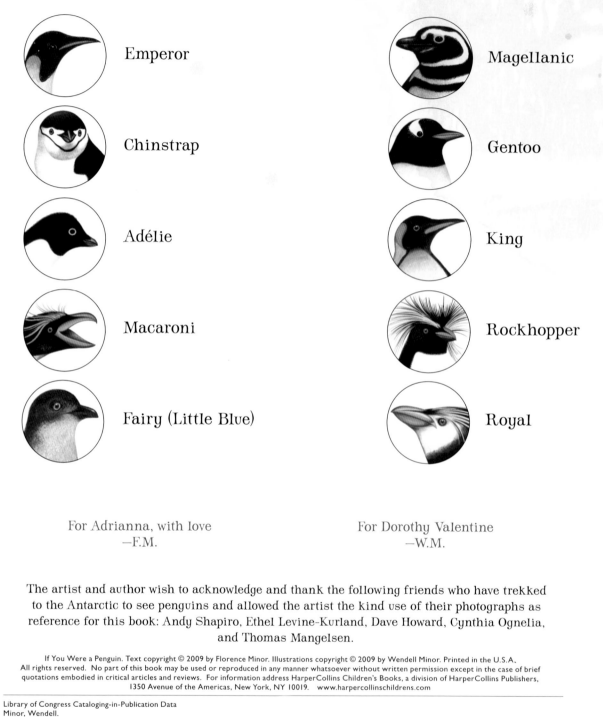

Emperor

Magellanic

Chinstrap

Gentoo

Adélie

King

Macaroni

Rockhopper

Fairy (Little Blue)

Royal

For Adrianna, with love
—F.M.

For Dorothy Valentine
—W.M.

The artist and author wish to acknowledge and thank the following friends who have trekked to the Antarctic to see penguins and allowed the artist the kind use of their photographs as reference for this book: Andy Shapiro, Ethel Levine-Kurland, Dave Howard, Cynthia Ognelia, and Thomas Mangelsen.

Library of Congress Cataloging-in-Publication Data
Minor, Wendell.
    If you were a penguin / Wendell and Florence Minor. — 1st ed.
        p.   cm.
    Summary: Pictures and rhyming text present some of the many extraordinary things penguins can do. Includes facts about penguins as well as related websites.
    ISBN 978-0-06-113097-7 (trade bdg.) — ISBN 978-0-06-113098-4 (lib. bdg.)
    [1. Penguins—Fiction.   2. Stories in rhyme.]   I. Minor, Florence Friedmann.   II. Title.
PZ8.3.M6467If   2009
[E]—dc22

2007021017
CIP
AC

Typography by Dana Fritts   2   3   4   5   6   7   8   9   10   ❖   First Edition